T0198644

EMMANUEL JANVIER

I'LL LOVE YOU UNTIL THE END OF TIME

authorHOUSE®

AuthorHouse™
1663 Liberty Drive
Bloomington, IN 47403
www.authorhouse.com
Phone: 1 (800) 839-8640

Published by AuthorHouse 01/18/2018

ISBN: 978-1-5462-2424-2 (sc)
ISBN: 978-1-5462-2423-5 (hc)
ISBN: 978-1-5462-2422-8 (e)

Library of Congress Control Number: 2018900535

Print information available on the last page.

The hardest thing to do is watch someone you love get hurt while you stand by helplessly.

—E. J.

Chapter 1

The first time Victoria Brown saw Steven Drake, he transcended every preconceived notion that she had of what the perfect man should be. It was as though a demigod had fallen from the sky and landed not too far from her grasp. She would watch attentively as he passed by, lacking the courage to utter a single word. As her days and nights grew longer, she became consumed by passion for this flamboyant young man, who seemed to have more on his mind than to notice a shy, frivolous young woman. When he didn't seem interested, she sadly abandoned all hope that they were meant to be. But fate works in mysterious ways.

One day while Steven was going to school, he heard an incessant giggling coming from the first-floor balcony of an acquaintance. He was curious to see who it was, so he lifted his head and saw one of the most scintillating faces he had ever seen. It was as though he had ascended to heaven and had seen the most beautiful angel that God had ever created. When he laid his eyes on her, his whole world came to a complete halt. He felt his heart racing at a pace that was uncomfortable. He experienced hot and cold flashes at the same time; he was—to state it in one word—mesmerized. As for Victoria, she was giddy as a schoolgirl who had just been asked to prom by the coolest guy in school. She didn't know whether to cry or laugh. All she knew was that she wanted this moment to last forever. But just when Victoria thought that Steven was about to proclaim his undying love for her, it was as though some mystical force pulled him away. And he left without saying a single word.

After a couple of days, she became worried because he had stopped coming by. She would repeatedly shout in her room, "Why didn't he tell me how he feels? Did I do something to offend him? Am I not pretty enough?"

She realized that all the questions could not be answered. She tried to pursue the matter further. Luckily for Victoria, her cousin, Frank Banditto, was a good friend of Steven Drake's. He practically knew everything that had happened to Steven because they grew up together. One day Frank noticed Victoria crying, so he asked her what happened. Reluctantly, she told him that she was in love with a young man and thought he would love her too, but as it turns out, he didn't. Now, Frank was the type of person who cared for his family and wanted to know who it was.

Finally, he dragged it out of her.

When she told him who it was, he said to her, "I am about to tell you something that not too many people know about Steven Drake."

She automatically assumed the worst. "If it's that bad, then I don't want to know," said Victoria.

"No! It's not what you think," said Frank. "You see, a long time ago, Steven Drake was known as a lady killer, but fortunately that was not true. He was only seventeen when he had his first sexual experience, and it was with an older woman named Rachel Donivan. That bitch turned Steven into someone he never was."

"But what does that have to do with me?" asked Victoria.

"Let me finish," said Frank. "Now, as I was saying, Steven was somebody who cared about school, but when Rachel came into the picture, she methodically changed his whole way of life. Try to understand: Steven was not working, he fell in love, and the combination of the two adds up to trouble. And at that time, he was not ready for all that."

"I still don't understand," said Victoria. "What do you mean she changed his whole way of life? Is he no longer interested in girls?"

"No! Not at all," Frank quickly replied. "He does not believe that he should ever let anyone get close to him, so the same thing does not happen again. Victoria, you are in too much of a hurry. Hear me out first."

As Steven explained, this woman seduced him and then became pregnant. When she realized that Steven could not take care of the child, she proposed to him that she would sleep with one of his friends and pretend that he was the father of the child. When she told Steven that, he did not know what to do. It was as if someone had stabbed him right through the heart. But since he was in love with her, he dismissed the notion. Another incident that occurred was when Steven heard a rumor that Rachel, the love of his life, had slept with another man. Frank told Victoria that the night he heard the story, he felt as if his heart was being slowly torn apart.

"He also told me that he felt a shooting pain and a burning sensation that could not be quenched by even a glacier," Frank went on to tell. "Steven cried himself to sleep that night hoping that when he woke up everything would be alright.

"Unfortunately, there was a big problem. Rachel was living with Steven's parents, meaning Steven could not kick her out nor could he leave, because he did not have anywhere else to go. As he told me all of these things, I thought, *You should never trust a woman*," said Frank.

"Is that all?" asked Victoria.

"No, there is more," replied Frank. "Remember—I told you that she was pregnant?"

"Yes, I do," Victoria said softly.

Frank started to explain to Victoria that Steven forgave Rachel, but there was still the matter of how he was going to resolve this major problem. "As I told you, Steven was not working, but fortunately Steven had a lot of friends, and when the chips were down, he confided in one of his closest friends, James Pierce, who lent him money so Rachel could get an abortion. After that first experience, something inside Steven died. He became an uncaring person. He built a wall around himself to prevent himself from getting hurt.

"When Rachel finally moved away, Steven breathed a sigh of relief. Even though he wanted to be with her desperately, deep down inside he knew they were never meant to be. The next few months were tough on Steven. He had many flings but nothing significant—well, maybe I shouldn't say *nothing* significant," said Frank.

"There was a young woman who I thought had rekindled what once sparkled within Steven. I can go as far as to say that he was beginning to break down the barrier he had built around himself. Her name was Jane Atkinson. She was not like Rachel. She was truly in love with Steven. Unfortunately, she was very jealous, and from the beginning, that was an impediment because Steven was not the type who sought out that type of attention. But he had fun with her ... or so I thought," said Frank.

"What do you mean?" asked Victoria.

"Well, according to Steven, she was nothing but trouble. He told me that she was so jealous that one day while at a party she tried to get him jealous by seducing one of his friends, and as soon as she did it, she reminded him of Rachel and all the bad feelings came rushing back to him. This time he had matured, so instead of falling to pieces, he got even and tried to seduce one of her friends. When she saw that she might lose Steven, she quickly apologized, and things were back to normal, but unfortunately they did not trust each other after that episode."

"So do you think that he loves me, and if he does, he does not want the same thing to happen?" said Victoria.

"Probably," said Frank. "Listen—I have to go, but don't give up. Maybe you are the person that Steven has been looking for. You never know—the third time could be the charm."

Victoria had finally found out why Steven did not tell her how he felt during their first encounter. How would she convince him that she was not like the rest? And besides, would she ever see him again? This question remained a bigger problem. For about three months, Victoria neither heard from nor saw Steven, so she started getting worried.

One day, by mere chance, she heard her father talking on the phone with a good friend whose name was John Drake. From the way they were talking, she surmised that this person might be related to Steven, so she asked her father, Richard Brown, who he was talking to. He told her that it was a good friend of the family.

"Does he by any chance have a son?" asked Victoria.

"How did you know he had a son?" demanded her father.

Finally, a glimmer of hope. If he has a son, it could very well be Steven, she thought.

That night Victoria could not sleep. She was happy to know that all was not lost. But how would she tell her father that she was in love, and better yet, would he approve? Whether he did or did not, if it was meant to be, then nothing in this world would keep her away from her betrothed.

The next day, Victoria's father told her that they were going over to the Drakes' home because he had told them about his daughter. When her father told her the news, she was full of anticipation. She fixed herself up as nicely as possible to go to the Drakes'.

When they arrived, she did not know what to expect, but she knew somehow everything would be all right. She met Anne Drake, Steven's mother, and John Drake, but Steven himself was nowhere to be found. Everything she had done was in vain, and again she thought she had missed a golden opportunity. But Victoria was determined to meet this elusive fellow one way or another. She wanted to make sure she had not fantasized about their first encounter. However, she was content just to know where he lived.

That evening, when Steven came home, his mother told him that his father's friend had come over with a charming young lady whom she thought was the type of person he was looking for, but Steven disregarded what his mother told him because he knew he had found his angel on earth already.

The following day Steven decided to pay a visit to his father's friend's house out of curiosity, and it was déjà vu all over again. That night, Steven, who usually was a talkative fellow, was unable to utter a single word. When Mr. Richard Brown tried to talk him about school, he became distant as if he was in another world.

Finally, when Victoria's father felt the tension between the two, he came right out and asked, "Is there something going on between the two of you that I should know about?" But since neither of them wanted anyone to know how they felt toward each other, both emphatically retorted that nothing was going on. So Victoria's father did not, for the moment, pursue the matter any further, but he was not in the least bit understanding. He grew up in a different time, and sometimes that makes for the worst parent of them all. But even though Mr. Brown did not understand, that did not mean he did not want the best for Victoria.

However, in the Brown's household, there was a major problem. For you see, Victoria was living with her stepmother, and she did not like Victoria because she claimed that Victoria's mother had taken her husband away from her. Joanne Brown made Victoria's life a living nightmare because she had several daughters of her own, and she'd hoped that one day Steven would marry one of them—not because she liked Steven, but because she knew he wanted to become a doctor.

In other words, she was trying to secure the well-being of one of her daughters through him. When she noted the attraction between Steven and Victoria, that added insult to injury. When Victoria became aware of what her stepmother was trying to do, she decided that she would take the initiative. One day she went through her father's phone book and called Steven.

"Hello," said Victoria.

"Hello," responded Steven.

"Do you know who is speaking to you?" asked Victoria.

"I'm afraid not," Steven replied.

"It's Victoria. I just called to tell you that I love you and want to be with you."

At that instant, Steven did not know what to say, nor did Victoria stay long enough on the phone to listen to his reply. *If all else fails, at least now he knows how I feel,* she thought, and she believed that in a matter of days, Steven would finally tell her how he felt. But after a day, a week, a month, there was no response. She thought that maybe she had scared him off.

But what she didn't know was that Jane Atkinson had not totally been out of Steven's life. Jane Atkinson and Steven Drake never formally broke up, but she did move away. When she came back, the first person she contacted was Steven. One day Steven heard someone knocking on his door, and when he opened the door, it was one of Jane's friends.

"You have to come with me. Jane wants to see you." Without hesitation Steven went to see Jane, and when he got there, he noticed she had been crying.

"Oh, Steven!" Jane exclaimed, her heart racing. "I've missed you so much," she said softly.

"Then why didn't you ever call me?" inquired Steven.

"I didn't call because I thought you would never forgive me for what I did to you," Jane replied.

"So why did you want to see me?" Steven asked impatiently.

"I wanted to see you because I want you to forgive me," Jane responded.

"If that's all you came for, then you're forgiven," Steven retorted coldly.

"I would also ask you for another favor. I want you to take me back," pleaded Jane.

"I could never take you back because the trust we had in each other no longer exists. And besides, I'm in love with someone else," Steven snapped.

"Who is it? I have the right to know," demanded Jane.

"Listen, it doesn't matter because you went as far as to make me jealous. I knew it was over, but I just did not want to tell you," he explained.

"I'll get even one day, Steven, and don't you forget it … I'll get even one day," she muttered.

"Maybe so, but for now, I'll have to take my chances," he added.

After that episode with Jane, Steven finally knew that he was truly in love with Victoria, and no matter what, he would pursue her until she was his. Steven decided that he was going to ask Mr. Brown for his daughter's hand in marriage, but little did he know what awaited him. At 7:30 p.m., Steven and his friend James Pierce went to the Brown's. When he arrived, he could almost taste the tension in the air.

"Good evening, sir," Steven greeted politely.

"Good evening, Steven," replied Mr. Brown.

"I have come to ask you for your daughter's hand in marriage," Steven blurted out nervously.

At first, Mr. Brown did not say anything. Then he asked, "Where are your parents?"

This was not at all what Steven had anticipated. "Well, maybe I came on too strong, but I just want you to know I love your daughter," he continued nervously.

In an almost inaudible voice, Mr. Brown snapped. "What did you say?"

Steven reluctantly repeated himself.

"Don't you know that she has a boyfriend?" Mr. Brown asked awkwardly.

"N-no sir! I didn't know that …" and before he even got to finish his sentence, Mr. Brown disappeared into a room and came back out with a picture of a young man who was supposed to be Victoria's current love interest.

"Here, this is all the proof you need," said Mr. Brown. "Furthermore, when you came here about a month ago, didn't I ask you if there was something going on between you and Victoria? Do you remember what you said to me?"

"I do, sir," muttered Steven.

"So then, what in the hell are you talking about now?" Mr. Brown lashed out.

At that instant, Victoria knew she was in for it.

"Victoria, come here," growled Mr. Brown. "What is going on? Do you want to explain what Steven is doing here?"

Victoria was at a loss for words. She knew that her father not only had a bad temper but would not understand. So to save herself from the grief, she simply told him that she did not know what Steven was talking about. When Joanne Brown, who was listening to the conversation, heard what Victoria told her father, she stormed out of the bedroom and said, "You're the worst liar on the face of this earth. Don't you know I heard you calling Steven a couple months ago to tell him that you loved him?" Victoria at that point could not say anything.

As for Steven, he felt like the biggest fool that ever existed. He left without saying another word. When Steven got home later that evening, he wanted to kill himself. How could I have been so blind? I should have known that she was engaged to someone else, *he thought bitterly.* This is the last time I'm going to let this happen to me. From now on I will never let myself become involved with a woman because it just doesn't pay in the end. *Even as Steven* thought these words, deep down he knew he didn't mean a single one of them. Meanwhile, Victoria was at an insurmountable impasse. How should she explain to her father what had transpired?

That night, Mr. Brown only gave Victoria a stern warning, but he told her the next time something like that happened, he would send her back to her mother. Unfortunately for Victoria, her father was the least of her worries. She was worried about how Steven was going to feel toward her now. She knew he had been betrayed by two women before, and she didn't want to be another to do the same thing. But no matter how she looked at it, it seemed that she had done exactly that.

The very next day Victoria woke up early in the morning to go to Steven's house to try to explain to him why she denied everything. When she arrived, Steven was on his way out the door.

"What do you want?" Steven asked.

"I came to explain to you why I acted the way I did," replied Victoria.

"There is no need to explain. I think your father said basically all that was needed to say," he concluded.

"You don't understand, Steven; I love you, I don't love the man my father was talking about anymore. You have to understand he was my first love, but ever since I met you that has changed. Haven't you ever loved someone before only to find out that you were attracted to someone else?" Victoria pleaded.

"Well, I can't say that I haven't," Steven replied.

"For me it's more that attraction, Steven; I truly love you and want to be with only you," admitted Victoria.

"If you only wanted to be with me, why didn't you tell your father that last night?" Steven inquired.

"I was afraid, but if you want me to tell him, if that will prove to you that I mean every single word—I will," replied Victoria.

"No, that's okay, I believe you. You don't always have to prove anything to me, but promise me no matter what happens we will always be friends even if we are not lovers," Steven said.

That day they promised to each other that they would be together sometime in the future. A couple of weeks later, Steven heard the most disturbing news ever. He heard that Victoria had been slapped by her father because she had come to see him. At first Steven did not know what to do. He felt rage toward Mr. Brown and love and pity for Victoria. It was as if someone had desecrated what he held dear. He thought he had to do something to rectify this insidious act as soon as possible.

"But what?" he said out loud.

He thought maybe if he were to go to Mr. Brown and explain the whole situation, then things might change.

"But how?" he mused.

From their last encounter, it didn't seem as if Mr. Brown wanted anything more to do with him. Nevertheless, he had to do something. Steven decided that before he went to Mr. Brown's house, he would call first. But then again, what good would that do? Would Mr. Brown even talk to him, and what would his parents say? They weren't aware of what was going on. Just as Steven was about to call, the phone rang, and it was Mr. Brown. In fact, he insisted on talking to John Drake, Steven's father. For a long time, the two of them spoke on the phone, and when they were done, Steven's father called him to the den. He told him what Mr. Brown had explained to him and said from now on he was to stay away from Victoria. Now Steven felt as if his whole world was crumbling around him. He wanted to tell his father to go to hell, but out of respect, he kept his silence. When Anne Drake heard the two arguing, she came into the den to find out what was happening. Then John told his wife what Steven said. Anne didn't say anything at first, but then she turned to her husband and asked, "Don't you think that Richard Brown is exaggerating? Steven has always been a fine young man, and I don't think he would intentionally try to insult Richard by going to his house and asking for his daughter's hand in marriage without being accompanied by us. Besides, Steven doesn't even know if she's engaged or not." As his mother spoke, Steven realized that his parents were just as rigid as Mr. Brown was.

"What do you mean? Do I need your permission to fall in love, too?" exploded Steven. "Would you have preferred I go behind his back with his daughter? I was doing the right thing, and besides, I am not a child anymore."

"Don't take that tone with me, young man. As long as you are living under my roof, you will do as you are told. I knew that girl was bad news from the moment I saw her," Anne scolded.

"Well, that's not what you told me a couple months ago—you thought she was my type," replied Steven.

But when Steven realized that if he continued with the argument it may bring more trouble for Victoria, he decided that he would no longer talk. For several hours, his parents talked, but he simply pretended they didn't exist. The only thing he could think about was Victoria. That night, a million thoughts ran through his mind. *How can I get even with that son of a bitch, Mr. Brown?* But Steven knew for that moment there was nothing he could do. He would simply have to leave it to the future for Mr. Brown to get what he deserved.

However, Steven was deeply concerned about Victoria because he did not know what kind of torture she was going through. He called Frank Banditto, Victoria's cousin, to keep him informed about what was going on. Steven realized he was no longer welcome at Mr. Brown's house even though Victoria's father had not specifically stated so. Frank became his liaison, and from time to time he would write romantic letters to Victoria, and she would do the same. They met secretly at times to talk about their uncertain future.

One day while they were together, Victoria asked Steven, "Why don't you want to make love to me?" Steven at first was silent, and then he said to her, "I believe we should wait because I don't want to ruin your future. Don't you ever imagine what would happen if you were to become pregnant and we weren't able to take care of the child? We'd be back to square one." Victoria knew he was right, but when a person is in love, he or she doesn't like to think about the consequences.

"I am willing to take that risk as long as I am with you," Victoria declared. When she said those words, Steven knew that this was the girl he was going to spend the rest of his life with, no matter what happened. "Victoria, I want you just as much as you want me, but we're not ready to take that step. Believe me, when we do it, it will be magical."

While Steven spoke to Victoria, he could not believe that these words were coming out his mouth. *You must be nuts*, he thought to himself. *The woman of your dreams wants to make love, and you're saying no. Love or whatever it is sure has changed you.* But deep down inside, he knew he was right even though he had those nagging thoughts. As they departed, Victoria asked Steven the most puzzling question: "Steven, do you ever think we will be together one day?"

"Of course we will, Victoria," he responded, but there was uncertainty in his voice. Steven knew that it was not impossible for them to be together, but there would be a lot of hurdles to jump before that dream finally became a reality. With that in mind, Steven started wondering what his next move would be. Should he drop out of school and get a job to support Victoria, or should he continue with his education and have Victoria wait for him? Both scenarios seemed feasible, but which one was the best? For all concerned this was something that Steven was going to have figure out in due time. And Steven had a feeling that he did not have too much time before something horrible happened. For about two weeks Steven heard nothing from Victoria, so he started getting worried. *What could have happened to her? I hope she's okay. If anything were to happen to her ... I don't know what I would do.*

When Steven could not shake off this dreadful feeling, he tried to contact Frank and ask him what was going on. When he finally reached Frank, Frank told him that somehow Victoria's father had found that they were meeting secretly, and he had beaten Victoria so badly that she had to be hospitalized.

"I knew something like this would happen. But what should I do? I'm not working, and if I quit school, I could destroy my future as well as hers," said Steven. "What hospital is she in?"

"I can't tell you," replied Frank.

"Why not?" Steven asked eagerly, awaiting a response.

"Don't you see it would only make things worse?" said Frank.

"Yeah, you're right ... I wasn't thinking," mumbled Steven. "But please tell her that it's all my fault, and no matter what happens, I will try with all my might to fix everything."

"I'll give her your message, Steven, but listen to me—don't do anything you might regret," said Frank.

"Don't worry, I won't," replied Steven.

But Steven only had one thought on his mind and that was to get even with Mr. Brown. One night as Mr. Brown was coming from work, Steven decided once and for all to confront him.

"Mr. Brown, I want to speak to you for a moment," Steven demanded, only showing half his face.

At first, Mr. Brown was afraid because he did not know what Steven's intentions were "Stay away from me, you bastard. I don't want any trouble," said Mr. Brown.

"I am not looking for any trouble. I just wanted to know why you've beaten Victoria," replied Steven.

"I specifically told her to stay away from you, and she disobeyed me, so I punished her."

"Well, sir, with all due respect, the next time you lay your filthy hands on her, I will personally kill you," Steven exploded, threatening Mr. Brown.

"I don't have to stand here and listen to you. Get out my way." In Mr. Brown's haste to leave, he tripped and cut his hand on a bottle. "You see what you've done," he said.

"I didn't do anything," replied Steven.

"You haven't heard the last of me. The only way I would approve of you and my daughter being together is when hell freezes over," Mr. Brown said viciously.

"I'm sorry, Mr. Brown. I didn't mean to hurt you," pleaded Steven.

"Get out of my way," exploded Mr. Brown. "Stay away from me and my daughter."

When Victoria got out of the hospital and heard what had happened, she fell more in love with Steven, as if that were possible. She wanted to thank him for what he'd done, but she knew if she were seen with him it would mean even more trouble for her. All she wanted to do was share a tender moment with him, even if it meant it would be the last time they ever met.

That very same weekend, Victoria asked Steven if he would come to her house because her father would be away on a trip. She was not going with him because she had not recuperated from the brutal beaten he had given her. Reluctantly, Steve agreed that he would come. Steven had a feeling he knew what Victoria's intentions were. That Saturday Steven told his mother he was going to go James's house to spend some time with him, but he actually headed straight to Victoria's house. When he arrived, Victoria looked as ravishing as ever, and all he wanted to do was make love to her, no matter what the consequences might be. He did not say a word to he—he just pulled her into his arms and embraced her passionately. Then he told her, "Do you know how long I've wanted to do that?"

"So why didn't you?" Victoria asked.

"I was afraid I would not able to stop myself," he replied.

"Steven, must you always be so logical … I want you and you want me, so why should we wait?" asked Victoria.

"We must not rush into anything that we might later regret," replied Steven.

Then Victoria's mood changed. "I don't understand you, Steven. You say you love me, yet you don't want to make love to me."

"Listen, my love, it's because I care about you, and I don't want to hurt you. It's true; I love you so much I would rather let you think whatever you wish then to hurt you. I know how it feels to have the person you love hurt you, and believe me, it's not the greatest feeling in the world," Steven explained.

As they were talking. they heard someone at the door.

"Oh my God! Could that be my father!" Victoria said hysterically.

Don't worry; we're just talking. We didn't do anything," said Steven.

"Do you think my father will believe that, Steven?" replied Victoria.

"He will assume the worst," stated Steven.

When Victoria answered the door, it was James, who was looking for Steven because Steven's mother had call to ask if Steven was at his house.

"How did you know I was here?" asked Steven

"Steven, anyone who knows you as well as I do would know exactly where to find you. We've got to go because I told her you were busy and would call her as soon as possible," James said.

When Steven and James left, Victoria felt that she had once again been cheated, but the next time she would not let him loose so easily. When Steven arrived at James's house, he hesitated to call his mother, thinking that she had somehow found out that he was really at Victoria's house. When he did call, she told him something that would change the two lovers' course forever. She sounded excited on the phone, so Steven asked her, "Is there anything wrong?"

"Everything is terrific," she said.

"Why?" asked Steven.

"Because we're moving."

Those were the last words that Steven heard. At that instant, he no longer knew what he was going to do. When he finished talking to her, he looked as pale as a ghost.

"What's the matter?" asked James.

"My parents are moving. How I am going to break the news to Victoria? Now that I've found her, I can't leave." *There must be a solution, it just isn't fair.*

Steven knew he had his work cut out for him. How was he going to tell her the news, and more importantly, how would she react? Later that night, when Steven arrived home, he tried to persuade his parents from moving, but all his logic went out the window because they had already put a down payment on the house that they wanted to buy.

The next day, Steven went Victoria's house to break the news to her.

"What in God's name are you doing here?" said Victoria.

"I know it's unwise for me to come here, my love, but I have some bad news," replied Steven.

"What is it? Did your mother find out you were here yesterday?" asked Victoria.

"No! That's not it. I'm afraid my parents are moving," Steven said nervously.

Victoria was stunned. She said nothing and began to cry.

"Don't cry, my love," he said.

"You don't understand, Steven. I have gotten used to you. I can't imagine life without you," she sobbed.

"I feel the same way, too! But remember I told you once that no matter what happens I will always love you and I will never abandon you," explained Steven.

For the time being, those words that Steven uttered somehow soothed the feeling of desperation that Victoria was experiencing. Those words gave Victoria enough strength to go on for a while.

But when Steven moved away, she simply lost all hope. The only time she was happy was when she spoke to him on the phone or when they secretly met. Even though she knew she was taking a big risk, it did not matter.

As for Steven, he was in no better shape than Victoria. He tried not thinking about her too much, but the more he tried, the harder it was to keep her off his mind.

Victoria and Steven felt like they were living in a nightmare, and to make matters worse, Joanne Brown, Victoria's stepmother, had started taunting her, making her life even more unbearable.

"Did you think he'd be yours? He has a bright future—why would he be interested in somebody like you?" But despite everything she told Victoria, Victoria never listened to her stepmother because she knew that Steven would one day be hers and his heart totally belonged to her.

Even though they had been separated by distance, their love was stronger than ever. However, the things her stepmother told her were starting to have an effect on her. She started wondering if Joanne was right because after all she did make the first move and he did ignore all her advances. Victoria started second-guessing herself, and in doing so, she fell into the trap that her stepmother had set for her. Joanne's master plan was to eliminate Victoria and bring Susan, Victoria's stepsister, into the picture. When Steven used to come over to her house, he had become friends with Susan, and that was reason that Joanne exploded when she realized that Steven preferred Victoria.

Susan Brown was a sickly young woman, and Steven felt pity and not love toward her, but sometimes parents misinterpret what they see if they think it will benefit their young. Susan was not to blame for her mother's ambition. She simply regarded Steven as a friend. But Susan was not oblivious to what was happening in the house when Steven used to come over. She noticed that there was always tension between her and her stepsister, Victoria. It wasn't Victoria's fault either; if there was anyone to blame, it was Joanne Brown.

Another problem that existed in the Brown's household was the fact that Susan was treated better than Victoria, and Mr. Brown made sure that Susan was treated better than Victoria. He made sure that Susan had everything she needed even though he and Susan were not on the best of terms. When Susan realized what her mother was trying to do, she became intent on helping the lovers. She knew she was taking a big risk, but it was worth it because Steven had been such a good friend to her. At first Victoria was a bit skeptical of Susan and her plan, but when she finally realized that Susan was on her side, she was very happy as well as thankful.

And the timing could not have been better because Mr. Brown had figured out that Frank was the liaison between Victoria and Steven. He confronted Frank. Frank did not deny it; Frank told him if he had to do it all over again, he would not change a thing. He believed that two were meant to be together and nothing could come between what they shared. When Mr. Brown heard his own nephew talking to him this way, he insisted that he, Frank, never set foot in his house again for as long as he lived.

As the days went by, Susan and Victoria became closer and closer, and slowly but surely, Victoria confided in Susan. They knew that to keep their father in the dark, they would have to be cunning. Since Victoria was denied phone privileges, Susan would call Steven, and while Victoria spoke to him, she would stand guard. If her mother or stepfather was approaching, she would alert Victoria. But it became more and more difficult for the two to keep on taking their chances in the house, for they knew sooner or later they would get caught. To protect her stepsister, Susan decided it would be better if they called Steven on public phones. Victoria's father had discovered that though he had forbidden Victoria from having any contact with Steven, she did anyway. He did not let her go out without being accompanied by someone. Susan was always willing to go out with her, and Mr. Brown had no idea what was really going on. When the two lovers wanted to meet, Susan took it upon herself to arrange everything. One day, while Victoria and Steven were together, they started talking about how helpful Susan had been in keeping them together.

"You know, I feel a little guilty," said Victoria.

"Why?" asked Steven.

"Because Susan has been spending all her time and energy to make sure that we are together," said Victoria.

"I know," replied Steven.

"Do you think she can be our maid of honor when we get married?" asked Victoria.

"Of course! If anyone deserves it, it certainly would be Susan. Without her, I don't know what would have happened to us," said Steven.

When Susan thought she had given the two enough time to talk, she came over to Victoria and said, "It's getting late; we really ought to go." Before Victoria left, she embarrassed Steven passionately and said to him, "Don't forget what we talked about." Steven promised he wouldn't.

On their way back home, Susan suddenly tilted her head back for a moment and began gasping for air. At first, Victoria did not say anything, but a few minutes went by and she was still in the same position. Worried a little, Victoria asked Susan if was everything okay, and Susan told her she was feeling this way because of the excitement of the day. When Susan finally felt normal, Victoria told her that she and Steven had decided that when they got married, she would be their maid of honor. Susan just smiled and said, "I hope I live long enough to be at the wedding."

"Why in heavens would you say something like that, Susan?" asked Victoria.

"Oh, don't mind me. I was just kidding," she replied.

Even though Susan had tried to reassure Victoria that she was feeling much better, Victoria knew that something was wrong.

That night, Victoria did not get a lot of sleep. She knew Susan was sick and there was nothing she could do about it. What made matters worse was that Susan was relentless in trying to help her in whatever way that she could, even at the expense of her health.

The next morning, Victoria heard an argument between Joanne and Susan. The two were talking about Victoria.

"Why do you treat her the way you do, Mother?" asked Susan.

"Listen, Susan—she's not my daughter. I have to secure your future. I don't care about her. I care about you," replied Joanne. "Lately you two have become close, and I don't know what's going on. You've been spending too much time with that little tramp. Has she been taking you to places that we don't want you to go?" Joanne said angrily.

"Of course I've been going out with her, Mother! She is my stepsister after all, and if I can help her, I will, and there is nothing you can do about it," replied Susan.

"Oh yes there is! I'll make sure that she is thrown out on the street. You already know how her father feels about her. All I have to do is tell him that she's a bad influence on you, and she'll be out the door so fast she won't even know what happened," she said bitterly.

"Well, Mother, all I can say is, if she goes, so will I," replied Susan.

"What has she done to you? Has she turned you against me?" Joanne said.

"No, Mother! You've done that," snapped Susan.

Joanne slammed the door and left in a fit of rage. After a while Victoria came out of her room crying.

"Why did you do it? I don't want you to get in trouble because of me. I know you want to help, but it should not have to be at your own cost," she said to Susan.

"Now listen to me, Victoria; I meant every word that I said. I consider you my little sister, and I'm not going to let anything happen to you as long as I live. My mother and stepfather are wrong—they are trying to keep you and Steven apart, and that's not fair. Just call me an incurable romantic." The two hugged for a moment and then Victoria said, "Thank you, Susan. I'll never forget what you did."

The next day Susan called Steven to let him know what had happened.

"Steven, I'm worried that my mother might try to do something to Victoria," said Susan.

"What gives you that idea? Because she suspects something?" asked Steven.

"I'm afraid she might get my stepfather to kick out Victoria," replied Susan.

"Where is Victoria?" asked Steven.

"She's right here. Do you want to talk to her?" asked Susan.

"I would appreciate it," said Steven. "Victoria, are you feeling okay?" Steven asked, hoping for a good response.

"For the moment, I'm okay, but I'm worried about Susan," Victoria whispered.

"What do you mean?"

"Well, she had an argument with her mother over me. Steven, I cannot talk over the phone. I have to see you, so we can talk."

The very next day, Victoria and Steven met to talk about what had happened between Susan and her mother.

"Steven, I'm afraid that Susan is going to get herself into a lot of trouble, and I don't want to be the cause," said Victoria. "Don't get me wrong … I appreciate her help, but she's so frail. I'm afraid something might happen to her. She's pushing it," explained Victoria.

"You have to let her help us for now, or we'll lose whatever chance we have for happiness in the future. Don't worry about her health," said Steven.

"I don't believe what you just said," exclaimed Victoria. "Would you jeopardize someone's well-being just so we could be together?"

Steven did not say anything for a moment, but then he took hold of Victoria, looked her straight in the eyes, and said, "I would go to hell and back just to be with you. I love you so much, and I can't imagine life without you. Don't get me wrong—I don't want to see anything bad happen to Susan, but as far as I'm concerned, you're the only one that matters in my life. Without you I'd have no reason to live."

When he finished speaking, Victoria took several steps back, turned her face away from Steven, and began sobbing.

"Why are you crying?" Steven asked earnestly.

"I'm crying for many reasons," said Victoria. "First of all, you just said something I'll never forget as long as I'll live, and secondly, I don't want anyone to suffer because of us."

Steven whispered in her ear, "Well, kiddo, no one said it was going to be easy, but in your darkest hour, just call out my name, and even if I'm on the other side, I'll come to your aid."

"You don't have to say anything, Steven. I know you'll do your best to try and make me happy."

Victoria left for home feeling a bit reassured but uncertain about what would become of her and Steven. When she arrived home, her father was waiting at the door for her.

"Where were you?" demanded Mr. Brown.

"I went to see a friend," replied Victoria.

"Well, since you have so many friends … I guess you could go live with one of them," Mr. Brown stated flatly.

"Are you throwing me out?" asked Victoria apprehensively.

"Well, what do you think? Pack your things and leave," snapped Mr. Brown.

"But I don't have anywhere to go, Father. Please! Don't do this to me, I'm begging you!" pleaded Victoria.

"It's too late; you should have thought about it before you went out!"

When Susan heard the two arguing, she came running out her room.

"What's going on?" she asked.

"Listen, Susan, this is none of your business. I have to do this for her own good," replied Mr. Brown.

"How is kicking her out for her own good? If she goes, then so do I!" exploded Susan.

"You know, at this point, I really don't give a damn; if you want to go with her, then you're free to do so," growled Mr. Brown.

Victoria turned to Susan and said, "Listen, I appreciate everything you're trying to do, but I can't have you suffer because of me. Don't worry, I'll be fine." She turned to Mr. Brown. "But remember, Father, one day you'll regret what you did today, and I hope I live to see that day."

Without another word, Victoria packed her belongings and left her father's house, not knowing where she would spend the night. Fortunately for Victoria, that very same night she met Kate Jacobs, who saw her crying and asked her what was wrong. When she started to explain to Kate what was wrong, Kate felt sorry for her and invited her to spend a night at her house. But she told Victoria that she had a husband and that she could not stay for too long because she didn't know if he would approve. When the two arrived at Kate's house, Kate explained to her husband, Sam Jacobs, Victoria's situation, and they talked for a little while. They decided there was no harm in letting her spend a night. At least Victoria had a roof over her head for the night. The next morning, Victoria called Steven to tell him what happened. When she told him that she was no longer living with her father, Steven was relieved, but at the same time he was slightly worried.

"How long are you planning on staying at these people's house?"

"I don't know, Steven; as long as I need to. They seem like a pretty nice couple."

"Why don't you come live with me?" Steven eagerly asked.

"You know your parents would not let me stay over there."

Steven knew that Victoria was telling the truth, so he didn't try to push it. He resumed talking about the current situation. "How are you going to support yourself?"

"Steven, you ask too many questions. Don't worry about me," said Victoria.

"Victoria, I'll find a part-time job while I'm going to school, and things will be just fine. You know I can quit school and find a job," said Steven.

"No! I want you to become somebody. Besides, your education should be your number one priority," said Victoria.

"Well, it used to be. But ever since you walked into my life, everything else pales by comparison," Steven declared.

"I know you want to help me, Steven, but the best way to do that is to finish school," Victoria told him firmly. He had no choice but to agree.

For the next few days, Victoria was not as ease while at the Jacobs' house. After a few weeks went by, she started getting used to them, and for a while everything was going well for her. She was able to see Steven whenever she wanted, she was going to school, and she had a part-time job. She thought to herself that there was a light at the end of the tunnel, but things began to fall to pieces. Whenever she called Steven, he didn't pick up the phone, and his parents refused to tell her where Steven was. This worried Victoria even more.

One day, Sam Jacobs invited her to go out with him. Without thinking that something may happen, she went willingly. She thought Sam considered her as a daughter, but he had something else in mind. That night, he waited until his wife had gone to work and took Victoria out, but when Victoria noticed that Kate wasn't coming home, she became worried. As the night progressed, she thought, *Maybe I misjudged him.* When they went back home, Sam started acting strangely. He kept asking her all sorts of questions, like, "Have you ever wanted to have an affair?"

Victoria told him that the thought never crossed her mind.

When she was ready to go to bed, he came into the room and told her that the night was still young and proposed that they do something unpredictable. Victoria still had no clue what he was talking about, but she finally realized what he was hinting at. Then a feeling of dread came over her.

Oh my God. This man wants to sleep with me, and there's nothing I could do about it. She remained calm, but she knew Sam wasn't going to leave without getting what he wanted.

"Mr. Jacobs, I'm not really comfortable that we're sitting here and talking like this while Kate isn't here," said Victoria.

"Don't worry, sweetheart. I'm not going to hurt you; I just want to be your friend."

"I would really appreciate it if you left the room," Victoria exclaimed.

When Sam Jacobs realized that Victoria did not accept his advances, he began to get upset. "Now, what's wrong with you? You're acting like a child. You're acting like you never had sex before."

"To tell you the truth, Mr. Jacobs, I don't think that's any of your business. And just for the record, I haven't. Now, would you please get out of my room?" asked Victoria.

"Don't you talk to me that way, you little tramp!" roared Mr. Jacobs and leaped on her. She tried to struggle, but the next thing she knew he was ripping her clothes off. She tried with all her might to push him off, but she couldn't.

"Now, you little bitch! I'm going to give you what you deserve."

Victoria pleaded with him not to do this, but the more she pleaded the more obsessed he became. And when he had finished, he told her if she whispered one word about what happened to wife or to anyone else, he'd make sure that her life was a living nightmare. To make matters worse, he would kick her out the house so fast her head would spin.

The next day, Victoria felt as though it had somehow been her fault. Since she no longer knew where Steven was, she called Susan to let her know what had happened.

"Susan, something terrible has happened to me," exclaimed Victoria.

"What is it?" asked Susan.

"Remember that couple that I was staying with?" Victoria started to cry.

"What about them?" asked Susan.

"Last night, that son of a bitch raped me."

"What are you talking about?" asked Susan once again.

"Kate's husband raped me."

"That bastard!" yelled Susan. "You know you can't stay there any longer because you'll never know when he'll try it again, and you definitely have to tell the authorities."

"I can't do that because his wife has treated me so well," insisted Victoria.

"Well, listen, I'm going to have to help you. You don't have a choice now. I have to help you," insisted Susan.

"But how are you going to help?" asked Victoria.

"Don't worry, I'll take care of everything," responded Susan.

Victoria did not know what Susan had in mind, but she knew that she wasn't going to let Victoria end up in the same situation that she was in, and she knew she could not go back to the Jacobs'.

Susan was determined to help Victoria. The first thing she did was notify the authorities of what happened, but they told her unless the victim was willing to come forward, there was nothing they could do. Susan thought that the next logical step was to call Steven and let him know what had taken place. But when she called the Drake's house, Steven's mother was a bit vague and reluctant to tell Susan the whereabouts of her son.

"Mrs. Drake, I've got to know where Steven is … it's a matter of life and death," said Susan.

"Susan, I know you've been a friend of my son for a very long time. Steven has been hospitalized," said Anne Drake.

"But what happened?" Susan inquired.

"Well, we knew something was wrong about three weeks ago. He was studying all night and not eating. He could no longer handle the pressure, and finally he had a breakdown," said Mrs. Drake.

"I can't believe it! Thank you very much for telling me," said Susan. At that instant, Susan realized she had a major problem. How was she going to tell Victoria that she Steven couldn't help her? How would she react, and what would she do? Susan felt so distraught and angry that she decided to tell the one person that she shouldn't have told what happened to Victoria. She called Frank and told him what had taken place. When Frank heard the news, he wanted to know where Sam Jacobs lived so he could have a talk with him.

The next time Victoria called Susan, she asked Victoria to give her the Jacobs' address. No sooner did Frank have the address than he went over there to confront the man who assaulted his younger cousin. When Frank arrived at the Jacobs, he pretended he had delivery for Mr. Jacobs. When Mr. Jacobs opened the door, Frank grabbed him by the neck and started strangling him.

"What are you doing? I don't even know you!" Mr. Jacobs managed to yell.

"But you know my little cousin. The one you raped, you son of a bitch," roared Frank. "I'm gonna kill you!" Frank punched him in the face and kicked him until he was unconscious.

"That will teach you to prey on innocent young girls."

As Frank was beating Sam, Victoria came running accompanied by Kate. Kate wanted to know why this young man was beating her husband.

"If you don't tell her, I will," said Frank.

Victoria started crying and told Kate that her husband had raped her two nights ago. Kate told Victoria, "You should have told me … we could have resolved this matter another way."

"I don't even know how my cousin found out about it. It wasn't my idea for him to come and beat your husband."

After a long discussion, they both decided it would be better if Victoria left the premises, and once again, Victoria was out in the cold with nowhere to go. After the incident took place, Victoria and Frank called Susan to find out where Steven was because Victoria realized that she really needed him. Victoria started to ask Susan if she had any information about Steven. She didn't want to say anything at first. Finally Susan broke down and began to cry. Victoria and Frank thought that it was because of what Mr. Jacobs had done to her. Then she started to explain to what was troubling her.

"Victoria, I have some bad news for you," said Susan. "Steven is sick and is in the hospital."

"What's wrong with him?" Victoria asked hysterically.

"I'm not sure! All I know is what his mother told me. He suffered a breakdown because he was studying too much," said Susan. "Victoria, you cannot blame yourself for what happened to Steven," said Susan. "You know how persistent he can be once he sets his mind on accomplishing something. He just went too far this time."

"Is this supposed to make me feel better? He did this because of me. And now I don't know what I'm going to do. I'm completely lost without him. I need him, and I don't think I can make it without him by my side," said Victoria.

"Well, I hate to tell you this, but you're going to have to go on without him for the time being," said Frank.

"I couldn't agree more," replied Susan.

"I know this nice lady who takes in girls who don't have anywhere to go. Would you like me to take you to her?" asked Frank.

"I guess I have no choice," said Victoria. "I'll go with you, Frank, and thanks for being there for me. You're one in a million."

Frank and Victoria went to Cynthia Black's house, where she hoped that she could somehow put the pieces of her life back together again. When she arrived, she was puzzled because she saw were girls of all ages. Victoria thought that Mrs. Cynthia Black must be an angel to sacrifice her time by helping all these needy girls. The middle-age woman invited Victoria into the dining room so that the two of them could speak, and when Victoria explained her story to Mrs. Black, she felt compelled to allow Victoria into her home. This time, Victoria was vigilant because she remembered what had happened at the Jacobs' and she was not about to trust someone without getting to know that person.

"I know you have many questions that you would like to ask me, but for now I think it would be better if you got a good night's sleep," said Mrs. Cynthia Black.

Victoria knew that Mrs. Black was right. She didn't argue and went to the room Mrs. Black had assigned to her.

The next few days Victoria began to feel complacent, and she slowly started to associate with the other girls. As time passed, she made many friends. One of them was Ashley Jones, who was at first glance was a very troubled young lady, but nevertheless became a close friend of Victoria. After a while the two became inseparable and confided in each other. They shared chores and did everything together. But one night, Ashley noticed that Victoria was crying. "What is wrong?" she asked.

Victoria told her that she was thinking about a young man that she loved and that he had gotten sick because he was trying to help her.

"Well, did you ever think about going to see him?" asked Ashley.

"I don't know if I can," said Victoria.

"But you have to try, because if I'm not mistaken, it seems to me you are hopelessly in love with this character," said Ashley.

For about a minute or two, Victoria did not say anything. Then she thought, Why not? I have nothing to lose. I'll call my stepsister, and I'll go visit him at the hospital.

The next day, Victoria called Susan to find out where Steven was. When Victoria arrived at the hospital, she felt relieved and sad at the same time. She did not know how she would react when she saw Steven, so she braced herself for everything and anything. Steven came out of his room, and at first he thought he was hallucinating. Then he said softly, "Victoria, is that you? Is that really you?"

"It's me, my darling. How are you? Have you been taking care of yourself?" said Victoria.

Steven hesitated for a moment and then said to her, "I'm doing just fine now that you're here." As he said those words, Victoria could not hold back the tears as they ran down her cheeks.

"Steven, why did you study so hard? I know you want to help me, but I did not want to see you end up like this," Victoria exclaimed.

"I know, Victoria, but I wanted to help you have a better life. Now it seems as if I've only made things worse. I want you to promise me that you'll go on with your life. I'm no good for you in here."

"What are you saying, Steven?" asked Victoria.

"I'm saying that maybe you should forget about me," Steven sighed.

"I can't actually believe that you would say that, Steven. Don't you know I think about you day and night? Besides, we promised each other that no matter what happens, one day we would be together," replied Victoria.

"I know, but you can't wait the rest of your life for me, and I've failed you," said Steven.

"Listen, Steven, I did not fall in love with you because I thought you were going to become a doctor one day. I fell in love in you because of who you are … what kind of person do you think I am?" insisted Victoria. "You don't think very highly of me if you are talking like this after all that we've been through. I thought you would know me a little better, but apparently I was wrong."

"Listen, I'm very sorry that I hurt your feelings, but you have to realize that what I'm saying is the truth. I can't support you. I'm no good to you anymore. So let's just end it right here and right now," pleaded Steven. "I have nothing more to say to you except goodbye and that I'll always love you."

Victoria left the hospital full of anguish after Steven told her that it was over. She didn't know what to do. When she arrived at Mrs. Black's house, Ashley sensed that something was wrong. "I know it's none of my business, but is something wrong?"

"You wouldn't understand."

"What do you mean? Do you think you're the only one who has ever gotten her heart broken?" asked Ashley.

"No, but I love him so much, and he treated me as if I never meant anything," responded Victoria.

"Did he give you a reason for breaking off the relationship?" asked Ashley, "and do you believe it?"

"Well, right now, I don't know what to believe. All I know is that I love him," said Victoria.

"Well, Victoria, I hate to tell you this, but maybe Steven is making the ultimate sacrifice by letting you go because he doesn't want to see you suffer. Think about it," insisted Ashley.

For a few minutes, Victoria sat in her room and contemplated about what her friend had told her. Then she thought, *Maybe Steven thinks he's doing the right thing, but I'm not going to let him go so easily.*

For the next couple of days, Victoria was in a daze. She knew that Steven did not want to hurt her, but another part of her found it hard to forgive him for what he had said. Two weeks after Victoria visited Steven, she decided to go visit him and reconcile, but when she went to the hospital, he was gone. She thought Steven went home, but when she called, his mother told her that he had moved to a friend's house in another state because he was too ashamed to face anybody after what happened. Victoria thought that Steven had really meant what he said, and sadly she realized that she had to continue with her life. She went back to Mrs. Black's house after she received the news, and she arrived there, Mrs. Black told her that she wanted her to meet someone. Victoria did not know what to make of this because she didn't think anyone knew where she was living. Mrs. Black introduced her to a man who must have been twice her age, and from the very first time she laid eyes on him, she had a morbid feeling. They sat around and talked for a couple of hours, but all Victoria could think about was what this man wanted with her.

He finally said to her, "My name is Christopher Thrope, and I'd like to tell you that from the very first time I saw you, I fell in love with you, and I want to marry you."

"You don't even know me, and it's not that I want to hurt you, but I already love someone else," she told him.

The stranger left it at that for the moment, but Victoria saw a determined look on his face as he said good night to her.

As he left, Victoria noticed that Mrs. Black was a little upset, so she wanted to know what was going on. The first words that came out of Mrs. Black's mouth were, "I'm very disappointed in you right now, Victoria. Christopher is a nice man, and he can provide the stability you need in your life right now. I don't know why you turned down his offer."

Victoria turned to Mrs. Black and replied, "Don't think I don't understand what you are trying to do for me, but I must be frank. I don't love him; my heart already belongs to someone else."

"Do you mean Steven?" Mrs. Black replied.

"Yes!" said Victoria. "But how do you know about him?"

"Ashley told me all about it, which is why I tried to introduce you to Christopher. I thought maybe he could take your mind off that young fellow."

Victoria felt uneasy discussing her personal life with somebody she barely knew, so she causally excused herself from the conversation. Mrs. Black was very understanding and didn't pursue the matter any further.

For the next few days, Christopher came to Mrs. Black's house more frequently, and the main topic of conversation between him and Mrs. Black was Victoria, despite that she was uninterested in him. He did not want to give up. When he came, he brought her gifts that she naturally refused. He tried to ask her out, but every time he did, she always had some excuse why she couldn't go. Finally, the Christopher and Mrs. Black came up with a scheme. If they could convince Victoria that they both had her best interests at heart, maybe she would agree to marry him. But how could they convince her when it was obvious that she was still clinging on to Steven? They decided to make Victoria think that Steven was married and then she would finally realize that it was all over … really over.

The two of them tried to find enough information about Steven as possible, but who would they consult? Mrs. Black knew that Ashley was Victoria's friend, but she did not know that they had become close, and she did not want to give Ashley any indication of what they were up to. So Mrs. Black decided to use diplomacy to obtain what she needed to know from Ashley. From time to time, she'd ask Ashley questions about Victoria's personal life, pretending she was worried about Victoria. Slowly but surely, Ashley was unknowingly feeding her the information that she needed. Through her conversations with Ashley, she learned that Steven had one true friend by the name of James Pierce. So one day when Victoria came home from school, she was told that James had called and left a message. The message was that Steven had gotten married. When Victoria heard this, her whole world was shattered. She asked Mrs. Black if James left his number, but she said that he left no number. Victoria felt abandoned and decided that all she wanted was revenge. She wanted to hurt Steven as much as he had hurt her. The two culprits knew that their plan had worked, and Victoria was at the lowest point of her life. That night Christopher came by and saw that Victoria was crying, so he asked her what was wrong. She told him what had happened, and he played on her emotions.

"If he really loved you like I do, he would never have done this to you. You have to see that I'm the one who really loves you," said Christopher.

"I guess you're right," replied Victoria.

"Then will you marry me?" proposed Christopher.

"I guess," replied Victoria.

And with those two words, an unholy matrimony was born through lies and deceit.

On the morning of her wedding, Victoria felt as if her whole world was coming apart. She was beside herself because she knew that she did not love this man that she was about to marry, but on the other hand, she thought that she was alone because the one person who told her he would never desert her had done exactly that. And if all else failed, she knew she would have some satisfaction when Steven found out that she too had gotten on with her life. Victoria's marriage to Christopher was a very simple ceremony. They went to the city clerk and exchanged vows. She was not terribly excited, as one would imagine—it was just another day as far as she was concerned.

When everything was over, she told Christopher that even thought they were together, she would never forget her one true love. And that made him uneasy because he knew that he had obtained her through lies and deceit. Christopher quickly arranged for Victoria to move in with him now that he was legally married to her, and from the beginning, Victoria knew she was going to have problems because Christopher was very protective. Whenever Victoria went out, he wanted to know where she had been. Whenever she was talking to someone he did not know, he wanted to know who that person was and how she knew that person. As the marriage progressed, she knew she had made a terrible mistake, but there was no way to rectify it now. After a couple of months, Victoria became pregnant, and as far as she was concerned, the pregnancy, although a blessing, had sealed her fate. Victoria gave birth to a baby boy, and for a long time he was the center of her universe. She made sure that the baby had everything he needed, but she also could not help but think if only he was Steven's child. *If only Steven had not done this to me.* The more she thought about her predicament, the more she grew to desire Steven. Christopher did not make it easy for

Victoria because instead for trying to be sensitive to her needs, he started to resent her for the fact that she was not willing to let go of Steven. And most of their arguments seemed to revolve around someone who was no longer a part of Victoria's life.

One day, Ashley called Victoria to tell her some startling news. Ashley overheard Christopher and Mrs. Black talking about how their plans to entrap Victoria had worked out remarkably well. When Victoria found out about the way she was tricked into marrying Christopher, she was furious. She thought that maybe she should divorce him, but then she thought about Christopher Jr., and that immediately stopped her from doing anything rash. She knew that if she filed for divorce, chances are Christopher would get custody of her child. She could not envision life without the most important person in her life. She knew sooner or later she would confront Christopher and demand to know why he had deceived her. Later that day, when Christopher came home, Victoria was more cold than usual, and he wanted to know why.

"Victoria, is something wrong?"

"You have the nerve to ask me if something is wrong after what you've done to me?"

"What have I done?"

"You lied to me! You told me that Steven was married so that I would marry you! How could you be so cruel? How could you?"

"Well, sooner or later, he would have been married. I didn't exactly lie to you—I just stretched the truth."

"What do you mean 'just stretched the truth?' You don't know anything about him!"

"I don't care! All I know is that he would have dumped you, so I just saved you the trouble."

"Well, thank you very much for ruining my life. Thank you!" she shrieked and ran out the room in tears. At this point, Christopher felt guilty for what he had said and done and tried to comfort Victoria.

"Get away from me, you bastard. I'll never forgive you for this."

For a long time, Victoria pondered over whether she and Steven were ever meant to be. Why did she meet him? Why was he taken away from her? Would destiny make them ever meet again?

As for Steven, he was miserable without Victoria. He moved away to try to let go of his memories of her, but the more he tried to forget about her, the more he was compelled to find out what became of her. One day, Steven got a phone call from James Pierce, his old friend, the only one who always stayed in touch with him.

"Steven, my friend, I'm afraid I have some bad news for you."

"What is it, James? Did something happen to Victoria?"

"Yes, I'm afraid so. She's married."

"Married! But how? To whom?"

"I don't know the whole story. Everything is sketchy to say the least, but I heard she was married," replied James.

When Steven heard this, he did not know what to do. He blamed himself because he thought that it was because of the way he pushed her away the last time he saw her. He had no idea what to say. *So she has decided to go on with her life. I guess I have no choice but to do the same.* Even though Steven had decided to go on with his life, there was still a part of him that regretted what he did. He still knew that he loved Victoria, but now there was nothing he could do about it. Reluctantly he sought comfort in the arms of another woman. Her name was Christine Johnson. She was a very beautiful young woman, but the only reason Steven was with her was because he felt terribly lonely and he needed someone, anyone, to help take his mind off his one true love. Unfortunately, Christine did not see it that way. She was in love with Steven, and she made it very clear to him. When Steven saw that she had serious intentions, he tried to let her know, but she did not want to hear it. What made matters worse was that Steven met her father, Phillip Johnson, who was a very nice man, and after a while Steven felt as though he was taking advantage of his daughter. It came down to either breaking off the relationship completely or giving marriage some serious thought.

One day, Christine invited Steven to have dinner with her. Steven accepted, and as they were eating, Christine asked Steven if he had ever thought about settling down. The first thing that came out of Steven's mouth was "Yes, I had thought of getting married," but when he realized where she was heading, he did not want to pursue the conversation any further.

"Steven, tell me, why didn't you settle down?" asked Christine.

"Well, I wasn't prepared. I wanted to make sure that I met the right person before making such a big decision," replied Steven.

"Have you met the right person?"

Steven hesitated for a moment and said, "I don't know."

Christine didn't pursue the conversation any further because she sensed that Steven was a bit uncomfortable. For a long time, Steven had not heard any news about Victoria. But one day, James called him again to tell him that Victoria had given birth to a baby boy. Once again, Steven was torn inside. He knew that there was only one way to prove to himself that he had gotten over Victoria. It was to get married, a reasonable act that he thought about very carefully. Finally, one day he invited Christine to go to the movies with him. At the movies, Steven kept asking himself all sorts of questions, like, *Should I ask her to marry me? Will I ever forget Victoria? Should I try to regain Victoria's love even though she's married?*

Logically, he knew what he had to do, but his heart was telling him something else. He also knew that there would be certain advantages to marrying Christine: her father was rich, and he would be able to finish school if he married her.

After a long internal debate, Steven came to the conclusion that there was nothing to lose. He decided to ask Christine to marry him. She was more than willing, and her father made sure that their wedding was one of the greatest affairs that had ever taken place. At Christine and Steven's wedding, there were several influential people in attendance. It was a storybook wedding, except Steven had an ulterior motive for marrying this beautiful young lady. Steven led the opposite life of Victoria. While Victoria had to struggle with Christopher to make ends meet, Steven had everything he wanted except his true love. He was living an opulent lifestyle. He felt miserable because although he did not know for sure, he had a feeling that Victoria was not very happy and there wasn't anything he could do about it.

Steven thought, *Maybe there is still another way to help Victoria.* If he couldn't give her love, maybe he could still help her financially. Steven started asking Christine for money, which he sent to Victoria anonymously. Victoria was able to have almost anything she wanted without really knowing who her benefactor was.

One day Christopher got curious and demanded to know who was sending his wife money. When he confronted Victoria, she told him that she didn't have the slightest idea, but of course Christopher didn't believe her.

"You better tell me who is sending you money."

"I don't know. Maybe it's my father—I don't know!"

"Why would your father send you money? He hates you!"

"I guess he feels sorry for me."

But Victoria didn't know that her father, Richard Brown, started having problems the moment that Victoria stopped living with him. Joanne realized that since Mr. Brown had rudely kicked out Steven as well, there was no way that one of her daughters would be able to get close to him. Because of that, she grew to despise her husband, and in the process, Victoria's father discovered why his wife had behaved the way she did toward Victoria. He felt guilty, but it was too late. When he heard Victoria married at an early age, that made it even worse. As their relationship deteriorated, Joanne made an awful mistake that sealed her fate in her husband's eyes. Richard Brown had someone close to him passed away, and his wife was hinting that she would entertain some friends because her youngest daughter was about to turn sixteen.

Richard was totally against it, and he specifically told her that during this time of mourning, he didn't think it was appropriate for his family to be celebrating. Joanne disobeyed him and decided to entertain a couple of friends in his absence. When Richard Brown returned and discovered that his wife had not listened to him, he became furious. He didn't want anything to do with her. Finally, after years of keeping silent about what he'd done to Victoria, Richard Brown exploded on his wife.

"Do you know that you've made me make the biggest mistake of my life?" he bellowed.

"What did you say?" asked Joanne.

"You've made me ruin my daughter's life because you wanted to secure the happiness of yours. I didn't realize it until you disobeyed me. That's when I knew why you were so against Victoria and Steven being together, and I didn't help matters either by being so bullheaded."

"Well, I didn't force you to kick her out. You did it! So don't blame me if you can't live with yourself," said Joanne.

"You know what; I can't take it in this house anymore."

"Well, if you can't take it, then why don't you just leave?" said Joanne.

"What did you just say?"

"You heard me!"

Richard Brown asked her if she was giving him an ultimatum, and she told him to interpret it however he wanted. As far as she was concerned, it did not matter one way or the other. Richard Brown, being a proud man, took his belongings and left. He rented a filthy basement and stayed there until he figured out what his next move should be.

A family friend told Victoria what had happened to her father. She was not at all happy, but she did feel that there was a God somewhere. Nevertheless, she felt obligated to help him. She went out of her way to find her father, and when they did finally meet, they had a touching reunion.

"Victoria, I'm sorry for the way I've treated you in the past, and I hope you'll find it in your heart to forgive me," said her father.

"Father, I don't blame you for anything," said Victoria.

"I know I was hard on you, Victoria, but believe it or not, it was because I loved you. I didn't want anything bad to happen to you," said Mr. Brown.

"I know, Father," said Victoria.

"And I am sorry I was against you and Steven being together."

Victoria knew that she could not leave her father in that apartment, so she asked him to live with her and her husband.

"Don't you think Steven will mind if I live with the both of you after the way I treated you?"

"I didn't marry Steven; I married someone else," said Victoria.

Richard Brown was surprised to discover that Victoria hadn't married Steven. "I thought the two of you would naturally get married after you ... I mean, after I threw you out of my house."

"Well, things happen," said Victoria.

"Is there a chance that you two might get back together again?"

"No, I don't think so! I don't even know where he is now, and besides, we didn't part on the best of terms. He thought it was best that we ended our relationship because he thought he wouldn't be able to take care of me."

"I know it doesn't matter anymore, but I'm sorry things didn't work out between the two of you."

"So am I," replied Victoria. "Father, I can't leave you here. You have to come with me, and I'll take care of you."

"I don't know, I don't want to impose," said her father.

"It's no trouble. Besides, you know I love you, and you're the only one I have left," said Victoria.

The first day Richard Brown met Christopher, he knew he was not going to get along with him. Maybe it was because of the way he reminded him of how he had treated Victoria in the past. Whatever it was, you could tell those two did not see eye-to-eye.

One day while Christopher was not around, Mr. Brown decided to talk to Victoria about her situation.

"You know, Victoria, you don't have to live like this. I can tell you're not happy. So why don't you just leave him? We are both working; we can rent an apartment together and share the cost!"

Since Victoria did not want to be in the marriage, her father had given her something to consider. But she still had reservations about the idea because even though she had forgiven her father for everything he had done in the past, it was hard to forget. And Christopher had something Victoria would die for— her only son. So she thought hard about taking any drastic measures.

Steven, however, continued with his schooling and eventually graduated with a degree. He thought, *Now that I have finished what I set out to do, it is time for me to reclaim the love of the woman I could not forget.* But he did not know how he was supposed to leave his wife, Christine. She had not given him any problems, and she also remained faithful to him through the years. He thought maybe he could reason with her. He didn't mean to deceive her, but his heart belonged to someone else. At first, Christine was devastated. She could not believe that Steven had used her that way. She wanted him out of her life, and she made it perfectly clear to him. Their breakup was very traumatic for Christine, and didn't part on good terms, but at least it was all over.

Steven decided he would return home and pursue, by any means, the woman who had been in his heart for what seemed like an eternity. When Steven returned, he discovered things were different. Victoria had given up hope; the young woman he had left behind was a stranger to him. When they reunited, the light that once flickered in her eyes was gone, and it was Steven's main goal to rekindle that passion for life that she once had. At first, Steven invited her to the movies, but she declined several times. He then asked her to go to dinner with him, and she still did not want to go.

One day, she invited him to her house, and Steven felt uneasy going to another man's home knowing all too well his intentions. He started to talk to Victoria, saying, "Listen, I'm not going to push you into making any decisions you're not comfortable with." But at that point Victoria was in, and she did not want to hear a sanctimonious sermon. She needed someone to take charge, to rescue her, and Steven still did not want to take charge. As always, he left it to Victoria to take the first step.

Days later, Steven and Victoria were alone in the apartment, and she started to cry hysterically. He asked what was wrong, and she told him that she blamed him for everything that happened to her and that for a long time she had hated him. She asked him, "Do you know how it feels to sleep with someone you aren't in love with? After a while, you just stop caring about everything."

"Well, I don't know," replied Steven. "How come you never contacted me?"

"What do you mean? When was the last time I saw you?" asked Victoria. "The last time I saw you, everything was over—at least that's what you told me!"

"Well, I'm sorry. I thought I was making the right decision for the both of us!"

"You were wrong! You abandoned me, Steven, when I needed you the most."

As she talked, he felt her pain. He wanted to comfort her, but something inside of him kept him from doing so. He knew she belonged to another person.

"What do you want me to do?" he asked.

"I want you to face up to your responsibility," declared Victoria.

"Just say the word, and I'll do whatever is necessary so that we can be together," insisted Steven.

Meanwhile, Richard Brown, who had been in the other room listening to the conversation, felt compelled to plead his daughter's case to Steven. He came out of his room and said to Steven, "I don't mean to tell you what to do, but I would like it very much if you thought deeply about what she said because I too know what it is like to feel abandoned and unwanted. Maybe I made mistakes in the past about you and my daughter, but now I see that she really loves you. You two were meant to be together."

Steven could not believe that this was the same man who told him years ago to stay away from his daughter.

That night, Steven went home to plan his next move. The following day, Steven went to James to ask him for advice. The first question that James asked was, "Do you really love her?"

"I've never stopped loving her. From the first day I saw her up until now I do."

Then James looked straight into his eyes and said, "Then why on earth do you need my advice? It's up to you to figure out what you're going to do because if you want something bad enough, you have to be willing to fight for it." While James was talking, the only word that stayed in Steven's mind was fight, and now he knew exactly what to do. Steven went back to Victoria's house two weeks later, and the first thing she asked him was whether he had come to some decision. For a moment, he did not say anything, and then he looked her straight in the eye and said, "Yes, I've decided that I want to be with you." Then he leaned in for a kiss, and the exact moment before their lips met, Christopher walked in. He demanded to know what in the world was going on. He told Steven to leave the house immediately because obviously there was more going on than he knew about. That's exactly what Victoria was waiting for. She sprung up and said, "How dare you talk to one of my closest friends that way! I think you should apologize for the way you've acted."

"He has no right to be here, and besides, it's disrespectful. I'm no fool. I know what he's after," said Christopher.

"Well, if you hadn't tricked me into marrying you, there would be no need for him to be here. You knew I didn't love you, and I made that perfectly clear to you," growled Victoria.

"Why? You ungrateful bitch. Where was he when you needed help?" asked Christopher.

"Now, wait a second, buddy. To begin with, she's not a bitch, and if you use that tone of voice or try to harm her in any way, you'll have to go through me," said Steven.

"Get the hell out of my house," demanded Christopher.

"I'm not going anywhere without Victoria. It's obvious she doesn't want to be here," shouted Steven.

"I don't know what you see in her. She's not rich. She's not the most beautiful girl in the world. So, why do you want her so bad?"

"Have you ever seen a rose that was on the verge of dying? If you decide to water it every day and not subject it to too much light, it will undoubtedly rejuvenate. That's how I see her, and that's something you will never understand because you are not used to something that is beautiful and delicate like Victoria," explained Steven.

"Well, if that's the way you feel about her, why didn't you stay with her?" Christopher asked eagerly, waiting for a response.

"I was a fool! If I had known that this is how her life would turn out, I would have never let her go," Steven responded.

"Listen, I don't want to hear your sanctimonious praises about Victoria. I want you out of my house. We could do it one way or another. You can decide to leave on your own, or you can be put out by force."

Steven knew that this time would maybe be the last time to ever stand up for the woman he loved, so he told Christopher that he was not taking another step without Victoria. When Christopher heard Steven's bold statement, he grabbed Victoria by the hand and hurled her toward him.

"Well, if you want her that bad, you can have her."

Unfortunately, Victoria landed inches away from Steven, and he could see that she was hurt. The next thing Steven knew, he was punching Christopher.

Everything that had happened in the past came rushing at him, and all he could think of was killing this man who had abused the woman he loved.

Victoria shouted, "Steven, please stop! I don't want you to go to jail!" But he was so enraged that he could not stop. Finally, Victoria said to him in a sweet voice, "Steven, I love you. Don't let him come between us. If you hurt him anymore, then he will win." Steven stopped and looked Victoria, starting to come back to his senses, but by that time, Christopher was barely alive. When Victoria saw that Christopher was unconscious, she called an ambulance, and as always, a patrol car was also dispatched. When the paramedics arrived, they wanted to know what took place, and it was obvious there had been a fight. Christopher was rushed to the hospital, and Steven did not deny that it was he who was fighting with him. And given the circumstances, he would do it again. The police had no choice but to arrest Steven on the charge of attempted murder.

While Christopher was fighting for his life at the hospital, Victoria worried about the fate of Steven.

"Steven, do you know what you've done? If he does not live, you might be facing the death penalty. Do you want to die? What possessed you to do such a thing?" said Victoria.

"Victoria, I know I was not thinking much, but when I saw him hurt you, I snapped. I could not control myself. I love you so much; I couldn't stand by and watch you get hurt. And if I had to do it all over again, I would not change a thing," responded Steven.

"I'm very happy that you care for me, but now look at what has happened to you. You are behind bars, and if he doesn't get well, you might be charged with murder. Do you think I want that on my conscience?" asked Victoria.

"Listen, it's best that we don't think about what might happen" said Steven.

"You still don't understand after all these years, do you? I want to spend the rest of my life with you. How will this be possible if you are sitting in a cell or worse if they decide to convict you for murder? If you die, you would take the best of me with you. I can't imagine life without you, Steven."

"Don't worry. Everything will be alright. Besides, I was trying to stop him from hurting you. Surely, the court will decide in my favor," said Steven.

The next couple of days Steven sat in jail awaiting arraignment, while Christopher's life hung in the balance.

Fortunately for Steven, Christopher got better little by little, and before long, he was out of the hospital. When he came home, the first thing he wanted to do was press charges against Steven, but he knew that if he did then Victoria would go to the authorities and explain to them why there was a fight in the first place. Finally, Christopher realized things would never be the same between him and Victoria. He decided to give her a divorce and did not pursue any legal action against Steven. Steven was relieved when he heard he had exonerated, but what made it even more worthwhile was the fact that Victoria was finally his.

For the next few days, the two lovers rekindled what they knew would never die. They took walks in the park together. They went out to dinner and to the movies. They were inseparable. But little did they know that their journey was far from over.

Someone in Steven's distant past came back to haunt him. It was Jane Atkison. She promised him that one day he would regret what he'd done to her, and that's exactly what she set out to do. She designed an elaborate scheme. She knew that James Pierce could always find Steven, so she went to James and told him that Steven had fathered her daughter. This of course was nothing but a ruse, but she knew that Steven would feel obligated to marry her. As soon as James told Steven the news, he became frantic and wanted to know where she had been. To care for his daughter, he wanted to contact her to make some sort of arrangement. The very next day, James called Steven and told him that he knew where he could go to get in contact with Jane. Without thinking twice, he knocked on the door, and Jane opened the door with a look of astonishment in her eyes.

"Steven, is that really you?" she said.

In a cold voice, Steven replied, "Yes! Now, what is this I hear about me being the father of your child?"

"Well, it's true! You are!" said Jane in an excited way.

"You know before we go any further, I want to take a paternity test just to make sure," insisted Steven.

"Why don't you believe me?" she said.

"Let's just say I'm not going to take your word for it."

"Well, if that's how you feel about it … don't come here anymore. If you don't trust me, then there is nothing I can do to change your mind."

"This has nothing to do with trust. I just want to confirm what you are saying. Being a father is a big responsibility, and if I'm going to be one, I want to make sure the child is mine."

When Jane heard what Steven had to say, she burst out in a fit of fury. "What the hell are you insinuating? Do you think I would make this up?"

"I'm not saying you're stupid, but on the other hand, I don't think that it would be wise if I took what you said on face value."

For the next few days, Steven was troubled by what had taken place, and he really needed some advice. So naturally, he turned to Victoria to guide him through his ordeal.

"Victoria, I have a problem, and I don't quite know how to tell you this. A long time ago, I was—or I thought I was—in love with a woman named Jane. Recently she came back from God knows where to tell me that I'm the father of her daughter. It's been so long that I don't know whether she's telling the truth. What do you think I should do?" asked Steven.

"Well, it's not up to me to tell you what to do, but I think you deserve to know whether this child is yours. The only way you will find out is if you take some sort of test," said Victoria.

"You mean a paternity test!"

"Yes, of course!"

"I had not thought about that," replied Steven. "I only wish I knew someone who could tell me more about the way she's been living or where she was living.

Then I could get some insight into what had really been going on," said Steven.

A few weeks later, Steven ran into one of his old friends who had left the state a while ago. He started talking about his situation to him. "Frank, do you remember Jane?" asked Steven.

"Of course, I remember her!"

"Well, a couple of weeks ago, she came back into town to tell me that her daughter is actually mine."

"Don't believe a single word, Steven. I never intended to tell you this, but I know where Jane was living and what she was doing. When I left New York and went to Boston, I found Jane there. Believe it or not, she was not pregnant. It was after she met Tony that she became pregnant. When Tony found out what he did, he left her, and she had to deal with raising a child all by herself. Now that she needs financial help, she is trying to make you believe that is your child," explained Frank.

Now Steven was ready for the next encounter with Jane. She approached Steven once again and demanded that he take care of his child.

"Why are you against me taking a paternity test?" asked Steven.

"Because you should believe me, Steven," said Jane.

"Jane, it just so happens that I know the whole sordid details of how exactly you got pregnant," said Steven.

"What are you talking about? Are you out of your mind?"

"At first, I was out of my mind for even thinking that maybe you were telling me the truth, but thank goodness for Frank, who knew exactly how you became pregnant and who the father is. He told me about your past life, and now you still have the gall to stand here and tell me that your daughter is mine. Get out of my life, you slut! I don't ever want to see you again."

When Steven told Jane he knew, she broke down and headed straight for the door, totally ashamed of what she'd done.

Once again, Steven thought his problems were over, but little did he know that they were just beginning. When Jane discovered that Steven was indeed in love, she tried to do everything in her power to keep them apart. One day she confronted Victoria in the street.

"So you're the bitch that Steven is in love with. The one he can't keep off his mind."

"Excuse me, but I don't believe I know you," said Victoria.

"No, but I know you, and if you don't leave Steven alone, whatever happens to you will not be my fault."

"Are you threatening me?"

"Take it however you want. I'm telling you that I love Steven, and I'm willing to fight for him. So just watch your back," said Jane.

"Listen, if you have anything to say, don't tell me, tell it to Steven," replied Victoria.

The very next day, Victoria went to Steven to tell him what had happened between her and Jane. When Steven heard what took place, he was full of anger and couldn't wait to confront Jane about it.

A few days later, Steven went to where Jane was living to ask her what was she thinking. When he arrived there, he met Yolanda, the little girl that Jane tried to pass off as his daughter. When he laid his eyes on her, he fell in love with her and could not tear himself away from her. Then something happened. Something that Steven did not expect. The little girl walked up to Steven and asked bluntly, "Are you my daddy?"

At first, Steven was shocked, and he did not know what his reply should be. He did not want to hurt the little girl's feelings by saying that he wasn't. On the other hand, he did not want to give her any false hope. Steven stared at the little girl for what seemed an eternity. Then he gently picked her up and said, "Well, I don't know whether I am your daddy, but if you ever need someone to talk to or tell your secrets to, you can call on me. When you're afraid at night, and there is no one there to comfort you, you can call on me. If I am not mistaken, all these things are what a dad is supposed to do, so in that case, I am your daddy."

When Jane heard Steven talking like that to her daughter, she was deeply moved. She turned her head so that Steven would not notice the tears trickling down from her eyes. Then she called Yolanda and said, "Sweetie, it's time to go to bed, and Steven, I need to have a talk with you."

Steven picked her up, kissed her softly on the cheeks, and said, "Good night, sweetie. Don't worry; you'll be seeing me more often. That's if your mother wants me to."

When the little girl had gone off to bed, Jane could no longer hold back her emotions. She started to cry, and Steven, being a bit puzzled, asked her what she was crying about.

She gazed into Steven's eyes, held his hand, and said, "I want to thank you for what you just did. Now I know you probably came here to badger me about what I did to Victoria. I want to tell you right off that

I'm sorry; I don't want to cause any trouble between the two of you. It's just that Yolanda never knew her father, and the only person I could think of who was kind and loving enough to be a father to her was you. That's why I went to Victoria and told her to stay away from you—Steven, my little girl needs a father, and you're my only hope."

Steven didn't know what to say. He felt flattered that Jane would even consider him, but he also was not about to leave Victoria to stay with Jane because of Yolanda. He felt compelled to help Jane in any way he could except being a full-time dad to her precious little girl. Steven saw that it was getting late, and he did not want to give Jane any false hope, but how could he shatter the dreams of an innocent little girl? He did not want to be the villain in the complicated situation. Reluctantly, Steven told Jane that he had something to take care of and that they would continue this conversation later. He left her home without giving a definite answer to what she had asked him.

That night, Steven did not get any sleep because he knew that sooner or later he would have to tell Jane something. But what exactly could he tell her, and what did he have to do to make her realize that what she was asking the impossible of him? He woke up the next day with what he thought was a solution to his problem. Why didn't he simply adopt Yolanda and do the best he could do to become a father to her without having to marry Jane? He was so thrilled about the idea that he could not wait to tell Victoria because she was very understanding and would probably agree that under the circumstances that was the best thing to do. When Steven arrived at Victoria's place, he noticed that she was not herself.

"Did you have a talk with that woman of yours?" asked Victoria.

"What woman?" replied Steven.

"Jane, of course"

"I did, and sweetheart, don't be upset. The only reason she acted like that the other day was because she needed someone to be the father of her child, and she thought that without you I would agree to it."

"That's the stupidest thing I've ever heard. We have our own family to start."

As soon as Victoria said those words, Steven realized that his idea was not so great after all.

"Victoria, I didn't know that your divorce was finalized," said Steven.

"Oh, it isn't! But I am just thinking about our future together because I know as soon as my divorce comes through you'll want to marry me, and we'll be together the way it was always meant to be."

"You know, I've been thinking Jane has the most darling little girl you have ever seen in your life," said Steven. Then he sighed, "It's too bad she doesn't have a father to take care of her."

"What are you trying to say, Steven? I know you have something on your mind, so just tell me, okay?"

"Victoria, I want to adopt Jane's little girl."

At first there was a silence that filled the air. Then Victoria calmly turned to Steven and said, "Are you out of your mind? Don't get me wrong, I'm happy that you want to do the right thing, but that little girl is not our responsibility, and besides, I don't want anyone to come between us."

For the next few days, Steven debated whether he should adopt the little girl against Victoria's wishes. Then finally he thought, *What would be so wrong if I did? I'm sure that sooner or later Victoria will realize it's all for the best.* He returned to Jane's house a couple of days later to tell her what he thought was the solution to her trouble.

When Steven arrived at Jane's house, he noticed a familiar face that he had wished not to see for the rest of his life. It was Christopher, Victoria's ex-husband; he immediately asked Jane what was Christopher doing there, and you could almost feel the tension brewing.

"Now I get the picture. You two planned this whole scheme. All along you wanted me to look like a fool, didn't you," said Steven.

"I don't know what you're talking about. Christopher is a longtime friend, and there was never any intention of breaking up his relationship with Victoria whatsoever."

But Steven was not even willing to listen to what Jane was saying. He thought, *This has been a master plan that they devised together to keep me and Victoria apart.* Then Steven said, "I remember there was a time when you said you'd get even with me. Well, I hope you are proud of yourself, because you have finally gotten your wish."

Jane could not yet understand what Steven was talking about. Then she said, "For the life of me … I just don't know why you're so upset. I have not done anything to jeopardize your relationship with Victoria. There were times I tried to scare her, but you know why now, so you really don't know what I'm talking about."

"Then what is Victoria's ex-husband doing here?"

"Victoria's ex-husband! I had no idea Christopher was Victoria's ex-husband. He never told me that he was married to her at all," said Jane.

"So what is he doing here?" asked Steven.

"Since you took so long in giving an answer about whether you would do what I asked you to do, I decided to ask Christopher if he would consider raising Yolanda with me. In all honesty, he has been a longtime friend of mine."

For a minute, Steven hesitated, and then he said to Jane, "You know I can't believe what I'm hearing. Because of you, I don't know if I have a chance with Victoria."

At first Jane was puzzled. Then she asked, "What do you mean?"

"I mean," said Steven, "that I proposed to Victoria that maybe I should adopt your little girl, and believe me, she did not take it as well as I thought she would."

"Well, Steven, in all fairness, I didn't pressure you into making any decision. I simply asked you a favor; you were not committed to do anything that you didn't want to do."

"Don't patronize me!" he said. "Because of you, I don't know if I have a chance with Victoria."

Meanwhile, Christopher wanted to put his two cents into the argument, "I know this is none of my business, but I believe from his actions, Jane, that this person you call Steven is simply irresponsible."

At his point, Steven had enough of Christopher. He ran at him like a madman, pinned him to the floor, and started punching him because there was still some bad blood between them. When Jane saw what was happening, she called the police. When they arrived, they stopped the two men from ripping each other apart.

"This is the second time I've had to put you in your place, you bastard. The third time you won't be so lucky!" exploded Steven.

Later that evening, Victoria received a telephone call from the police department. At first she was not sure who it was intended for, but as the operator mentioned Steven and Christopher, she knew that somehow those two had gotten themselves into trouble again. When she went to the station, the two men were ashamed of what they had done, but Victoria was especially angry with Steven. She did not know what to say to him, and most of all she wanted to know why he was at Jane's house after they had concluded it was for the best that he stayed away from her.

As the two drove back from the police station, Steven said to Victoria, "Boy, you sure can pick 'em. How in the world did you end up with that excuse for a human being?"

At first, Victoria didn't say anything. Then she looked at him with glaring eyes and said, "How dare you talk to me that way? Did you really think I wanted to be with Christopher? Don't you try to put the blame on me.

"If there is anyone to blame, it should be you. You were the one that broke up with me, remember! I didn't have a choice at the time. I met him. I was young and naïve. I fell into his trap, but I'll be damned if I let you make me feel that I've done something wrong," said Victoria.

When Steven realized that he had struck a nerve, he quickly said to her, "I know how you feel. I'm trying to forget because believe it or not I feel guilty that I let these things happen to you. If I had known that things would've turned out this way, I would have never left you."

"Well, it's a little too late to apologize. What we have to do now is pick up the pieces of our lives and try to make some sort of order out of this whole mess.

"By the way," Victoria continued "you never did tell me what you were arrested for and why you were at Jane's house."

Steven knew he had to come clean because sooner or later Victoria would find out why he went there. "I went there to propose to Jane that maybe I should adopt her little girl, and Christopher had to put his nose in my business once again. So I put him in his place."

When Steven told Victoria why he went to Jane's house, she was beside herself with anger.

"I thought we agreed that idea of yours was not beneficial to either side. Didn't we talk about this, Steven? Didn't we?" asked Victoria.

"I know, and I heard what you said, Victoria, but I've got to follow my heart, and I believe that I can be a good father to that little girl," said Steven.

"And what about when we have our own children? What are you going to do then?" asked Victoria.

"Well, I don't particularly see it as a problem," said Steven.

"And do you think that Jane is just going to hand over her child to you?" replied Victoria.

"Well, we won't know until we ask her!"

"You know, Steven, I've really been trying to understand why you're trying to do this, and it dawned on me. Maybe you still have feelings for Jane."

"Don't be ridiculous. I don't feel anything for Jane. There's only one woman that I love and it's you."

"Are you sure, Steven?" asked Victoria.

"Yes! With all my heart," replied Steven.

"Then prove it. Forget this nonsense" said Victoria.

"Look, let's not fight about this," said Steven.

"I don't want to fight with you, Steven, but sooner or later, you're going to have to make a choice because you can't have your cake and eat it too," said Victoria.

"I need time to think, Victoria. This is not an easy decision."

"What is there to think about? Listen, have you forgotten that I too have a child? If you want to be a father so badly, why don't you start with mine?" insisted Victoria.

"You know I can't do that, Victoria. Even though Christopher is not on my favorite persons list, he does care for his child. After all you went through when you were young, surely you must know how important it is to have a father who cares about you."

"Yes, that's true, but I also know how important to have a real mother in your life, and unfortunately for me, my stepmother paled in comparison to my real one."

"Now, what is that supposed to mean!"

"It means I think it would be better if Yolanda grew up with her real mother."

Steven knew that Victoria was speaking from experience. So for the time being, he kept his silence. Then Victoria told Steven that she had some good news. She had finally gotten her divorce, and she wanted to know what he was planning on doing. For a moment, Steven did not say a word. For the first time in his life, he wasn't sure about what he should do because it was obvious that Victoria did not want to raise another woman's child.

Later that night, when Victoria returned home, she had an unexpected visitor. It was Jane, and she had come to Victoria's house to gloat, or so Victoria thought, but to her surprise, Jane came to apologize about the troubles that she had brought to Victoria's happy life. Jane told her some disturbing news about her ex-husband Christopher.

"Victoria, I did not want to be the one to tell you this, but Christopher went to the doctor the other day, and he was diagnosed with a rare cancer and only has about six months to live. He told me this in secrecy; he wants to spend what little time he has left with you, but he told me he knew it was over between the two of you," explained Jane.

"I don't believe you. Why are you doing this to me?" asked Victoria. "Isn't it enough that you have tried to trick Steven? Now you want to do the same thing to me. Just do me a favor and leave me alone."

For the next couple hours, Victoria did not know what to do. Things with Steven were not going well, and now this news turned her world upside down. That night, Victoria did not get any sleep. She knew that she had to do the right thing, but if she did, it could mean losing the only person she ever loved. There was no way that Steven would ever forgive her if he even thought that she was considering going back to Christopher, no matter what the circumstances were.

The following morning, she called Steven, and by the sound of her voice, he knew something was wrong. He decided to go to her house to find out what was troubling her. When he arrived, she was crying, and Steven thought it was about the fight that they had the night before.

"Victoria," said Steven, "I've been thinking maybe it's not such a great idea that I should adopt Jane's little girl. I think it's about time I concentrate on what matters, and that's you."

Then she said the strangest thing to him. She said, "You know, Steven, now I understand why you were so persistent in trying to do the right thing. It's not right that I should tell you what to do or what not to do. I understand much more clearly now." Steven was shocked.

"So what are you saying, Victoria? You don't mind if I adopt Yolanda?" asked Steven.

"No, I don't! Because it's the right thing to do," she replied.

"This is terrific!" said Steven.

"But before you ask, I want you to know that I would do anything for you. You know that—don't you, Steven?"

"Yes, I know, Victoria, but can I please finish because I'm about to burst if you don't let me ask you," said Steven.

Then he knelt on one knee and pulled out a beautiful engagement ring, and Victoria could hardly speak. He took her left hand and placed the ring on her finger. She looked at him with loving eyes and then he said, "My love, I know you've been waiting for what seemed like an eternity, but will you do the honor of becoming my wife?"

She turned away for a moment and started to cry. Then she said, "Steven, I have dreamed about this day since the first time I saw you, and if it were up to me, I would marry you in a heartbeat. But things change. For now, I can't."

Steven was stunned when he heard that she was not able to marry him.

"Well, what are you saying Victoria? You don't love me anymore?" asked Steven.

"Oh no! Steven, I love you more than life itself, but sometimes we have to make sacrifices even though it could mean our own happiness is placed in the back burner."

"But I don't understand. I thought you wanted to become my wife. What changed your mind? Is it because I was persistent in trying to adopt Yolanda?"

"No, darling, that isn't it. I have something to do, and no matter how I try to explain it to you, you would never understand."

"Listen, we have never kept any secrets from each other; no matter what it is, we will face it together," said Steven.

"No, my love. This is something I have to do alone," replied Victoria.

For the next few weeks, Steven tried everything he could to find out what it was Victoria had to do, but unfortunately, he did not find out anything. Then he heard the strangest thing from Jane. Jane told him that Victoria was planning on returning to her ex-husband and that was why she didn't want to marry him. But of course she conveniently left out why she was doing it.

When Steven heard this news, he was enraged. He told himself that he wanted nothing more ever to do with Victoria. Jane seized the opportunity to try to convince him that it was her all along who cared for him, and he should forget about Victoria. But no matter what she did, he would not get involved with her because he had not forgotten what she had done in the past. But even though he heard that Victoria was planning on reuniting with her ex, he had to see it with his own two eyes and to be convinced.

One day, Steven went over to Victoria's house to find out if indeed she had reconciled with Christopher. When he rang the bell, Victoria came and opened the door for him. It seemed as though she did not want to let him in, but when he went to the living room, he did not see anyone, so he thought to Jane had done it again.

"She is forever trying to keep us apart," said Steven.

Then to his surprise he heard a male's voice coming from the bedroom. It was Christopher. Steven immediately became angry.

"What the hell is he doing here?" called out Steven.

"I can't tell you, Steven."

"Are the two of you back together again?"

Christopher came out the room and said, "You did not really think she would leave me."

Steven did not even acknowledge his presence.

"Victoria, I'm speaking to you. Tell me that I'm imagining this," said Steven.

"I'm sorry, Steven … I've decided that for the sake of our son it's better for all parties that Christopher and I should be together."

"What are you talking about?"

"Look, Steven. This is what you've always wanted. Now you're free to do what you want to do," said Victoria.

Then Steven took Victoria by the arm and said, "Now, I'm going to get to the bottom of this. Look me in the eye and tell me you love him more than you love me, and I'll never bother you again." At first Victoria was hesitant, but she mustered every ounce of strength in her body, looked him right in the eyes, and with tears dripping down her cheeks, she told Steven, "I love him more than … I love you, Steven! I always have, and I always will."

Then Steven turned his face away from her as though disgusted by what she said.

"So if that's the way it is, then I guess we have nothing to say," said Steven.

"I guess not," replied Victoria.

Then Steven turned to the door and started to walk away. He heard her start crying louder than she ever had before. But he never turned back to look at her. He opened the door and left.

When Steven got outside, he felt as though everything he had ever done in his life was for nothing. As he walked away, he looked back once as if to say, "I don't know why you did this to me, my precious one, but always remember I'll love you until the end of time."

Printed in the United States
By Bookmasters